Evincepub Publishing

Evincepub Publishing

Parijat Extension, Bilaspur, Chhattisgarh 495001
First Published by Evincepub Publishing 2021
Copyright © Dipika Saha 2021
All Rights Reserved.

ISBN: 978-93-5446-116-3

Kindness is

Magic

BE THE REASON SOMEONE SMILES TODAY

DIPIKA SAHA

Author's Note

This is my first book. I am 13 years old and I love writing books and expand my imaginations. It's my first experience of writing a book and publishing it. I relied upon certain films that inspired me to write **"Kindness is a Magic"**. The eight stories that I have written will surely touch your heart and might inspire you. To all my readers: Hope you would like my first book. READ ON........

Illustrator

I am 9 yrs old and I love to illustrate pictures with my sister, Dipika who is the author of **"Kindness is Magic"**

– ARADHYA SAHA

Contents

1. Behavior Proves Your Soul..1

2. Overcoming Fears..4

3. Love Is Life..7

4. Mom Your Touch Is More Than Enough......................10

5. Mother's Love...12

6. Daddy Lies..15

7. A Simple Act Of Caring..19

8. Dirt Brings Glow...23

Behavior Proves Your Soul

An old, greybeard was cleaning his grocery store in the early morning. The street was quite busy, people running here and there and buying their essentials.

An old man noticed a lunatic, penniless boy sleeping just near his shop. The old man shouted "Hey! Stupid, silly move from my place". He kicked him away like a packet full of rubbish. He was an evil, heartless and a harsh man who did not want to look upon that boy for Yonce. One way or the other he tortured him a lot. He would pour water on him, yell at his ears and gave him unbearable pain. But the penniless could not utter a word; he used to sit and cry out of *immense pain and hunger.*

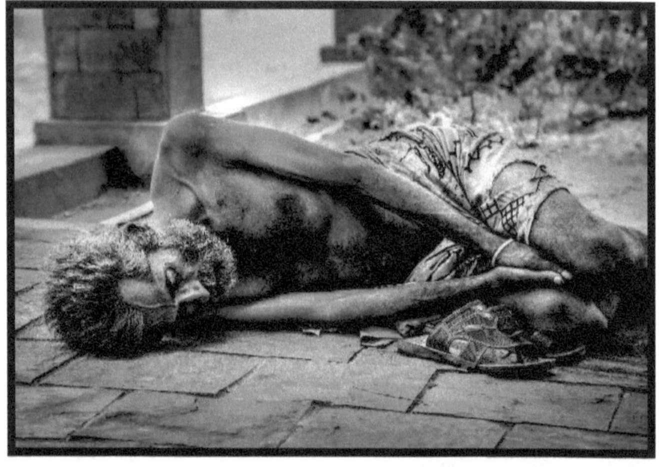

But one day a miracle occurred. Early in the morning as usual the man was cleaning his grocery store but he did not notice the maniac. He asked the shopkeeper next to him "Do you know where that fellow is?" "O that fellow! He is dead sir." The old man was astonished, "But how?" Sir two notorious thieves were trying to steal from your shop and he wanted to save your shop from robbery but he could compete with them so he was tortured and murdered. The old man broke into tears and felt extremely guilty about how he had behaved with the person and tortured him every day. The boy cared and protected his shop all night with all his strength. He apologized to god, "Forgive me! Though I have done an unforgiveable crime".

"Never ever misbehave with anyone, not even animals. God will always look into your deeds and award you the way you deserve."

Overcoming Fears

Each and every person on Earth has fear on something or the other, so this story that I'll narrate will be about overcoming fear and deciding it as a career.

In the cold city of "Lickzini" lived a little girl named Ziva. She was very scared of animals. Ziva's neighbor, Mrs. Maclin had a dog named Popo who used to guard her house. Popo used to bark at Ziva and she used to run away in fear.

After few months, the owner of the dog died due to oldage. The dog sat hopelessly and did not eat any food for days. Ziva used to feel extremely sad seeing the dog. With some courage she went near the fellow and kissed him on his head. The dog looked innocently at Ziva. From that day they became the best friends. Ziva gave it a good bath regularly with lots of care, tied a cute locket to him, played, ran and made him eat with lots of kindness. She used to take the black, furry one with her to the bus stop to catch her school bus. Popo used to wait there until Ziva came back.

But one fine day when Ziva leaped out of the bus she couldn't see Popo, instead she saw a large crowd. She ran and entered into the crowd and she saw Popo crying in pain, blood streaming out of his legs. She quickly cuddled Popo in her arms and ran to the veterinian but Alas! The vet centre was closed. Ziva with her shivering voice yelled, "Help me! Help me!" No one heard her cries. She had the most painful heartache.

A few years later after completing her higher studies she became a famous veterinian. Every time she cured an injured dog she used to remember about the memories she made with Popo.

"The things that give us fear, make us frightened can also lead to success. Do not get scared of anything. God sent you in place which is yours, you have the power to control every situation."

Love now days is just cheating, flirting and many other scams, well earlier it use to become a legend in the history like Romeo/Juliet and other inspirational characters who sacrificed their lives for maintaining a long term relationship. This love story proves an inexpressible love between an innocent girl and helpless boy.

It was a cold winter morning Lana was in her basketball practice. After half an hour when her practice got over she got in a taxi and was returning home. Soon a boy entered in her taxi and sat next to her, they both fell in love......This was though a flashback of what happened about three years ago.

Lana and Steve knew each other really well. Every day they used to chat with each other and call on phone. But one day Steve did not gave any response and he broke up. Lana knew that something was wrong. She called Steve but he did not picked up his phone. That night Lana couldn't sleep. Whole night, she only thought of her love. But the next few days when Lana kept on calling Steve, he received the call and asked Lana rudely, "Why are you calling me? I am nobody" and disconnected the call. She asked herself, "What did I do?".She was heartbroken and depression surrounded her with negativity.

One fine day, when she was driving her car to buy her groceries she was thinking about her memories she spent with Steve. She was not concentrating on her driving and got hit by a car. She was affected very badly. She was admitted to the hospital and Steve came to about her accident. He ran to a hospital terrified and sweating in intense sadness. After Lana's treatment was done

Steve ran to her room and by holding her hands letting her feel safe, he said," I love you Lana, I did not mean to hurt you ,I am affected by a deadly cardiovascular disease so I didn't wanted you to worry about it." Lana could not hold her tears anymore and they hugged each other and cried. With a throat tightening voice they told each other that they'll never leave each other alone in any circumstances.

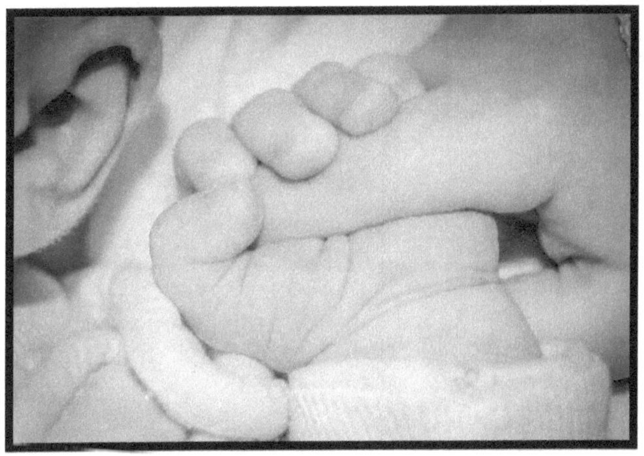

"LOVE is not finding someone to live with. Its finding someone you can't live without" if you are being loved by someone you are blessed and also a lucky person. Love a person and show that you have a beautiful heart"

Mom Your Touch Is More Than Enough

Who doesn't like those cozy hugs that mother gave when one was young? Every mother instinctively knows how to hold her baby from when she cradles her baby in her arms, to the way she strokes her baby's head. The physical act of touching ones child is a natural expression of the kind of love only a mother can give. She was standing in the kitchen looking at the window-sill and feeling guilty about her. She felt that she was not doing enough for her baby. Her infant was sleeping in the cradle next to her crying aloud. But did the cry reach the mothers ears? No, it didn't. Want to know why? Because she was a deaf and dumb woman. Neither could she talk to her baby nor hear its cries. But the moment she felt that the baby had some trouble she used to get scared and ran to the baby to help. The moment she touches her baby all the troubles around flies away and those two innocent eyes stares at the mother. She tells her baby from her heart, dear I didn't hear your first cry as I am deaf nor can I speak to you as I am dumb. I try to make you feel loved and safe and I try to say' I love you'. The baby with its two rosy, tiny hands wiped out tears of her mother. The bond between a mother and child is inexpressible and doesn't need words to express.

"Mom you may feel guilty that you are not enough but the touch that heals every single trouble is not replaceable." RESPECT YOUR MOTHER. *She'll care for till her last breath, so don't hurt her.*

Mother's Love

A mother and child relationship demonstrates love even in the face of conflict. It is an intense, special bond that is instrumental in lives of both.

Kaveri, a fruit seller used to live with her ten-year-old daughter Kithira in the mountains of Uttarakhand. They lived in a small hut in the top of the mountains. They had a tough time travelling up and down the hills. Kaveri used to wake up early in the morning just after sunrise. She used to send Kithira to the school and hurried to the market with her fruit basket. She had a great talent. She could cut fruits like pineapples, carrots, cucumber in different creative shapes resembling doll, toys, flowers etc to attract the customers. After school

Kithira used to help her mother in cutting fruits, she also used to learn the art from her mother sometimes she used to have minor injuries. She worked very hard all throughout the day. Kaveri could also make fruit ice popsicles which kithara saw her friends licking delightfully.

One day Kithara had a wonderful idea. She told her mother to make these fruit popsicles so that she could sell it in the market. Her mother felt that it was a wonderful idea and agreed with her. At first no one bothered to buy her fruit popsicles. Kaveri felt that the advertising was not appropriate so she made an advertising board with the price written. She cried out to call the passersby and try out her ice pops. Soon a huge crowd surrounded her to buy her ice pops.

She worked really hard and when she grew up she became a successful I.P.S officer. She never forgot how much support, love and encouragements she got from her mother.

"Someday when my pages of my life ends mother will be the most beautiful chapter of all".

The unconditional love and the sweet bond between a father and his child is inexpressible. It conjures up vision of limitless support of advocacy, protection absolute and beautiful love. They often lie to us to make us feel happy and satisfied. They never tell us about the sacrifices that they do everyday only to see a smile on their Child's face.

"Bye Daddy" five year old Emmy bid a goodbye to her daddy and entered the school. All was good but when daddy use to come to take her from the school, Emmy felt like saying, "Daddy why do you look so tired?" He stammered" Oh! Nothing. Actually the scorching heat of the sun made me tired" "Want to have an ice cream?" he asked Emmy. Emmy jumped in excitement. She got her favorite ice cream and hoping; jumping holding daddy's hand she reached home. Daddy used to do all the house chores and also made yummy dishes for Emmy. Daddy used to take Emmy to the park and played with her but lies can't be hidden.

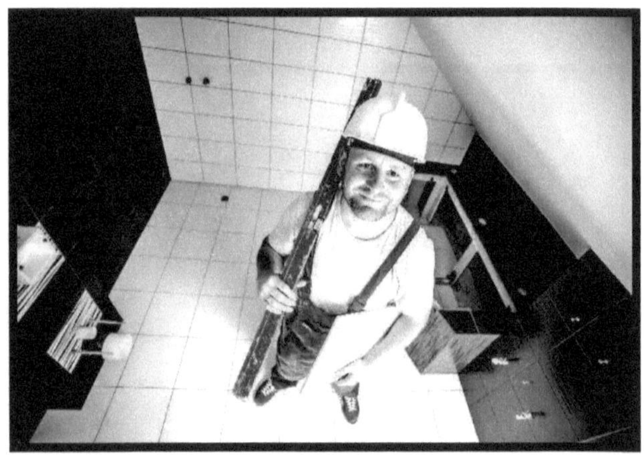

Emmy's school holidays came over. After a day or two, Daddy asked," Emmy, you stay at home I need to go to my work" "Daddy why did you lied that you were not hungry, why did you lie that you can afford me everything, why did you that you have time to play with me?" You work like a donkey every single day, sweating and tired, you carry huge loads on your shoulders, you sit with fruits in the market."

Daddy I have a small gift for you, "She read a note aloud," Dear daddy, you are my superhero, my inspiration, my idol, my Love and my best friend." Daddy I can't watch you working tirelessly like you do then she ran and hugged him and they both couldn't hold their tears. After knowing that Daddy works so hard for her she also worked very hard and she became top in class.

A person who never buys branded clothes, shoes, or perfumes and lives a simple life so that you can afford all of them. A fathers tears and fears can't be seen, his love unexpressed but his care and protection remain as a pillar of strength throughout our lives.

Some people are there in this world who knows that kindness is something that brings happiness and smile to thousands of people.

Chinki cried to her grandma, "Can we buy this yummy pack of chocolates? "No" Grandma Said.Chinki's heart broke. Grandma asked Chinki to buy something special for Grandpa as it was his birthday. Chinki quickly ran to the cake store, with an innocent heart, being superb excited she chose a chocolate cake which was Grandpa's most favorite. Chinki asked the shopkeeper," Uncle, can

I buy this cake? "Why not dear"? The shopkeeper said.

In a sudden all that pink, rosy smiling lips became sad. Grandma told, "Sorry dear, I can't afford it right now, buy something else. 'But its grandpa's birthday cake, you also said that you can't buy, the previous time. With her eyebrows lowered and pulled closer, with her eyes full of tears and with a gloomy face she was about to step out of the store. The man in the billing counter ran and asked for the same cake to the shopkeeper, 'I'll buy it" he said. He ran to the girl and offered her the cake."This is for you, take it and enjoy grandpa's birthday" the man said. 'But grandma can't pay 'said Chinki. '' I am giving the cake as a gift, you don't need to pay me a single penny" Her smile was like a sudden beam of light illuminating the darkest corner of the room. Grandma asked, "Who are you?"

"First let me tell you a story", the man said. When I was small just like Chinki I asked my mother to buy me a cake on my birthday. But the same way she couldn't afford me the cake. I cried a lot, seeing that a man in the queue whom I have never ever seen before, bought the cake for me and wished me a very happy birthday. The man continued," mistress you asked me, who I am, if I say that I am the man in the queue? Old grandma blessed the young man and thanked him for his kindness.

Chinki was very excited. She ran to Grandpa, hugged him and she handed the cake. "Why did you spend so much money on buying this cake?"Asked grandpa. Grandma said," A kind hearted man bought it for you and gave this note". The note says," *A simple act of kindness can bring ripples that comes back to you.*"

Grandpa was the man in the queue who gave the kind man a cake when he was a kid." Sometimes miracles are just good people with kind heart, no charm sparkles brighter than that of a kind hearted soul." It's very true you know, "A man with a good heart is worth more than a man with a good bank balance".

Do we like dirty, nasty things? No, we don't right? But would you like a story about dirt?

The story will make you change and you'll never feel dirty if you see a man wearing dirty clothes or doing their daily work with dirty things. You never know how pure their hearts are even if they have a dirty appearance.

Five little children came out after their school got over. Their mothers were waiting for them but there was something that suddenly made them annoyed. The kids were full of sticky mud stains all over their uniform. The mothers scolded their children. One of the mothers asked "Don't you know I don't like you to be filthy?" They thought that the children had surely done something naughty while the school was going on.

But a few moments changed their reactions. The principle came out of her room and smiled. She said, "Isn't it easier to remove the stains than it is to bring up a child.' She pointed at the CCTV Camera and said." Parents watch these small scenes of what your little ones did".

An old gardener was cleaning his clay pots and he had put those pots on a trolley and was pulling it over the wet grassy playground. Unable to balance the trolley due to old age it overturned and all the clay pots fell down. A small girl saw everything from far and ran to help him, she helped in settling everything. Soon, another four kids joined her and lend him a hand. The children were full covered with mud stains The gardener felt worried and concerned about the little ones and asked "I am sure you all will get a good scolding from your mothers." The children replied," No problem. Mothers always scold"

The mothers were overwhelmed. They never expected that those little children could help someone in need with a heart full of kindness. Watching the scenes the principle smiled and left the place.

"Kindness is a gift that everyone can afford to give"